R2003703358

W9-DFC-293

Beagles

Kate Riggs

CREATIVE EDUCATION
CREATIVE PAPERBACKS

seedlings

Published by Creative Education and Creative Paperbacks
P.O. Box 227, Mankato, Minnesota 56002
Creative Education and Creative Paperbacks
are imprints of The Creative Company
www.thecreativecompany.us

Design by Ellen Huber; production by Christine Vanderbeek
Art direction by Rita Marshall
Printed in the United States of America

Photographs by Alamy (GROSSEMY VANESSA), Dreamstime
(Igorr, Petr Kirillov, Marazem, Soloway), iStockphoto (GlobalP,
Halfpoint, phudui), Shutterstock (Akitameldes, AnetaPics, Art
Phaneuf Photography, dezi, IrinaK, Eric Isselee, Erik Lam,
MaraZe, Napat, Igor Normann), SuperStock (Jens-Christof
Niemeye/imageBROKER)

Library of Congress Cataloging-in-Publication Data
Riggs, Kate.
Beagles / Kate Riggs.
p. cm. — (Seedlings)
Includes bibliographical references and index.
Summary: A kindergarten-level introduction to beagles,
covering their personalities, behaviors, life span, and such
defining features as their tails.
ISBN 978-1-60818-661-7 (hardcover)
ISBN 978-1-62832-246-0 (pbk)
ISBN 978-1-56660-675-2 (eBook)
1. Beagle (Dog breed)—Juvenile literature. I. Title. II. Series:
Seedlings.

SF429.B3R54 2016
636.753'7—dc23   2015007562

CCSS: RI.K.1, 2, 3, 4, 5, 6, 7; RI.1.1,
2, 3, 4, 5, 6, 7; RF.K.1, 3; RF.1.1

First Edition HC 9 8 7 6 5 4 3 2 1
First Edition PBK 9 8 7 6 5 4 3 2 1

TABLE OF CONTENTS

Hello, beagles!

The beagle is a breed of hunting dog. It has a good sense of smell.

Small beagles
follow their
noses everywhere.

They are curious dogs.

Tricolor beagles have three colors of fur. Their straight tails point up when they run.

A beagle's ears are long and soft.

It has a smooth, rounded head.

Beagle puppies love to play. They like to be with people.

A pet beagle can live for 12 to 15 years.

Happy beagles run.

They sniff the
ground. Then
they curl up
to rest.

Goodbye, beagles!

Picture a Beagle

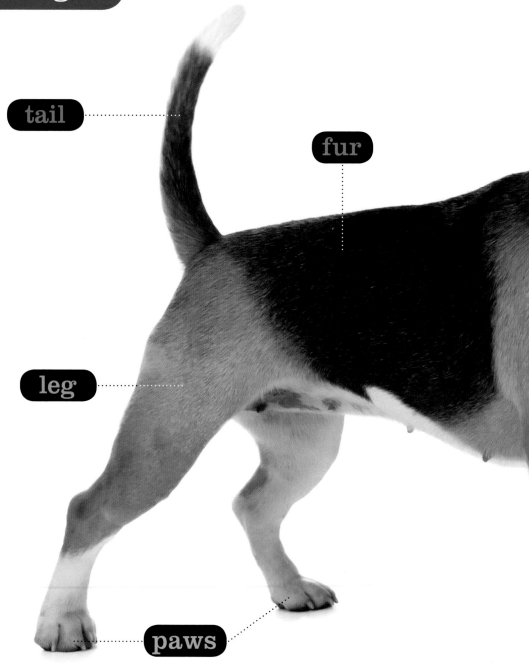

tail

fur

leg

paws

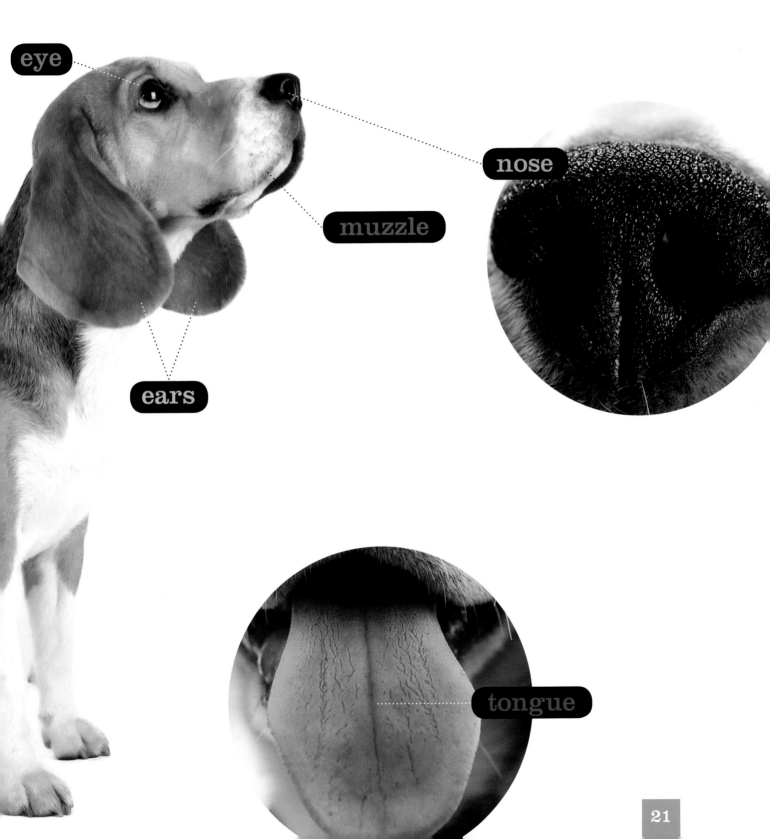

eye

nose

muzzle

ears

tongue

21

Words to Know

breed: a group of dogs that are alike

curious: wanting to know more about something

fur: the short, hairy coat of an animal

Read More

Green, Sara. *Beagles*.
Minneapolis: Bellwether Media, 2009.

Johnson, Jinny. *Beagle*.
Mankato, Minn.: Smart Apple Media, 2013.

Websites

Bailey's Responsible Dog Owner's Coloring Book
https://images.akc.org/pdf/public_education
/coloring_book.pdf
Print out pictures of pet dogs to color.

Beagle Video
http://www.animalplanet.com/tv-shows
/dogs-101/videos/beagle/
Watch videos about beagles and other dogs.

Index